**To Ann,
my favorite dance partner**

—R.W.

To my daughter Julieta

—A.L.E.

Text copyright © 2001 by Rick Walton
Illustrations copyright © 2001 by Ana López-Escrivá
G. P. Putnam's Sons,
a division of Penguin Putnam Books for Young Readers,
345 Hudson Street, New York, NY 10014.
G. P. Putnam's Sons, Reg. U.S. Pat. & Tm. Off.
Published simultaneously in Canada.
Printed in Hong Kong by South China Printing Co. (1988) Ltd.
Designed by Semadar Megged.   Text set in Triplex.
The art was done in acrylics on paper.

Library of Congress Cataloging-in-Publication Data
Walton, Rick. How can you dance? / Rick Walton; illustrated by Ana López-Escrivá.
p. cm. Summary: Rhyming text explores the many ways one can dance,
like the leader of a marching band, like a crab on a sunny day,
like a tree as it waves in the breeze. [1. Dance Fiction. 2. Stories in rhyme.]
I. López-Escrivá, Ana, ill. II. Title. PZ8.3.W199Ho 2001 [E]—dc21 99-24691 CIP
ISBN 0-399-23229-X
1 3 5 7 9 10 8 6 4 2
First Impression

hello

How Can You Dance?

Rick Walton

illustrated by Ana López-Escrivá

G. P. Putnam's Sons • New York

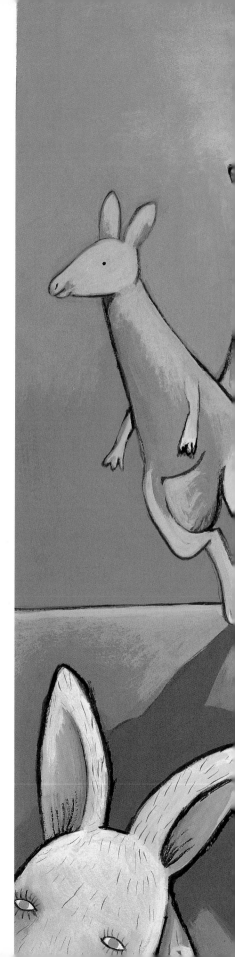

How can you dance when
Spring is in your shoes?
Dance like the king
of the kangaroos.

Bounce, bounce,
bounce, bounce,
Bounce, bounce,
bou———nce!

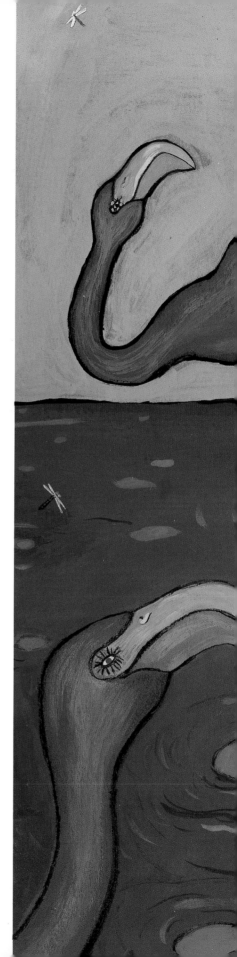

How can you dance when
one foot's sore?
Dance with the other foot
touching the floor.

Dance on the other foot.
Spin on the other foot.
Hop on the other foot.
Dance, spin, hop!

How can you dance as
you swim in a pool?
Dance like a frog
feeling fine, keeping cool.

Arms, legs,
Pull 'em in!
Push 'em out!
Pull 'em in!
Push 'em out!

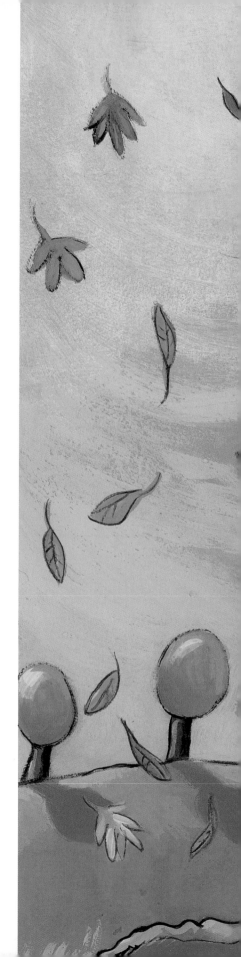

How can you dance when
you can't move your knees?
Dance like a tree
as it waves in the breeze.

Wave your arms wildly,
Round and round all over.

How can you dance when
you dance with your ma?
Dance like you're king
of the cha-cha-cha.

One
Two
One two three
Move those feet
And follow me.

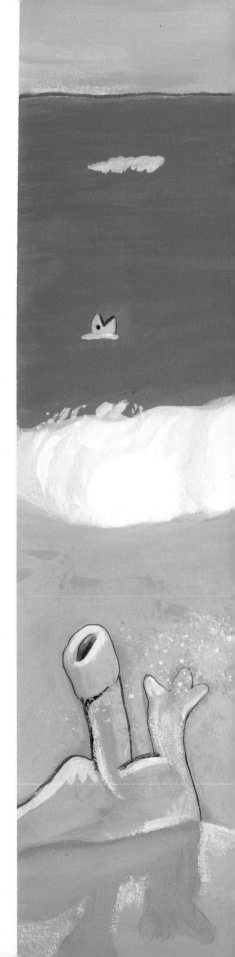

How can you dance when
there's something in your way?
Dance like a crab
on a sunny day.

Side-step-side
Look around
Side-step-side
Then dig in the sand.

How can you dance when
you're full of fear?
Dance like a fox
when the dogs are near.

Run away quickly,
Run away home.
Run away,
Run away,
Run!

How can you dance with
a stick in your hand?
Dance like the leader
of a marching band.

Keep in step now,
One, two, three, four,
Keep the music playing.

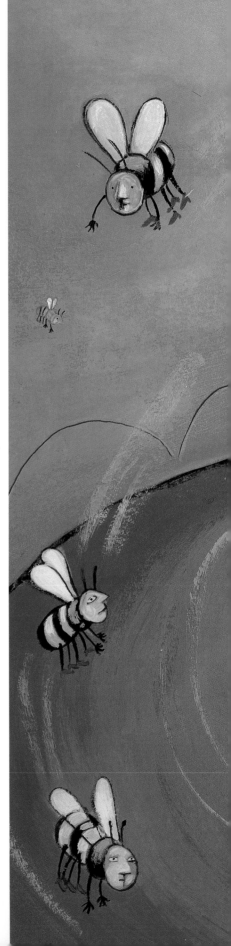

How can you dance when
you're ~~mad as~~ look like a bee?
Dance around, ~~around, around—~~
wildly.

Spin and run,
Spin and run,
Stop and sting
Everyone.

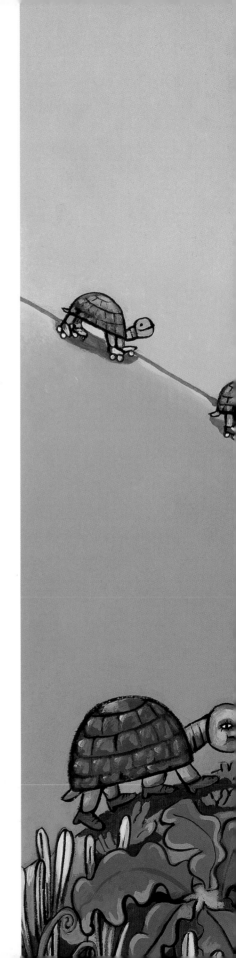

How can you dance when
you hurt your back?
Dance like a donkey
carrying a pack.

Slowly, slowly,
Can't move quickly,
Maybe I'll lie down.

How can you dance if
you're lying on the floor?
Dance like a snake
as it slithers to explore.

Wiggle, twist, glide,
Wiggle, twist, glide,
Stick out your tongue
and hiss!

How can you dance when
it's time to say, "Good-bye"?
Dance like a cloud
as it floats through the sky.

Drift away,

   wave so long.

      Drift away,

         Good-bye.